# Jack & the Ghost

CHAN POLING

# JACK & THE GHOST

with illustrations by

LUCY MICHELL

University of Minnesota Press

MINNEAPOLIS | LONDON

I thank my sister Julie Poling, who has been a great support during my first foray into this sort of thing and who introduced me to Dawn Frederick and Erik Hane at Red Sofa Literary. Many thanks to you guys. I also thank Erik Anderson and the team at the University of Minnesota Press; Jim Vick for making Lutsen and the North Shore a part of my life; and Lucy Michell, whose artistry and heart I admire so much and without whom I couldn't have proceeded. —Chan Poling

Thank you to Chan, for writing such a beautiful story and trusting me to illustrate it; Dawn Frederick and Erik Hane of Red Sofa for believing in this project; Erik Anderson at the University of Minnesota Press for bringing it to life; and Paul Guthrie and Kristie Sande for letting me stay in your northern Minnesota home in Two Harbors. Thank you to Jill, Richard, and Alice Michell, Jean and Bob Dooley, Claire and Elizabeth Lienesch, Sally Wingert, Tim Danz, Truman Danz, Krista Braam, Lauren Kebschull, Luke Borkenhagen, Wyatt Danz, Peyton Ashlei, Clara Iwaszek, and Geoff Freeman for supporting my artistic efforts and caring so dearly for my kids. —Lucy Michell



Published by the University of Minnesota Press
111 Third Avenue South, Suite 290
Minneapolis, MN 55401-2520
http://www.upress.umn.edu

ISBN 978-1-5179-0571-2

A Cataloging-in-Publication record for this book is available from the Library of Congress.

Printed in Canada on acid-free paper



24 23 22 21 20 19 10 9 8 7 6 5 4 3 2 1

*For my amazing Family. All of them.*

—C. P.

*For Cooper, Otis, and Arlo*

—L. M.

SSALY

The November storms on the great lake could be deadly.
When the ferocious gales blew across that vast seething sea,
the waves reached tremendous heights.

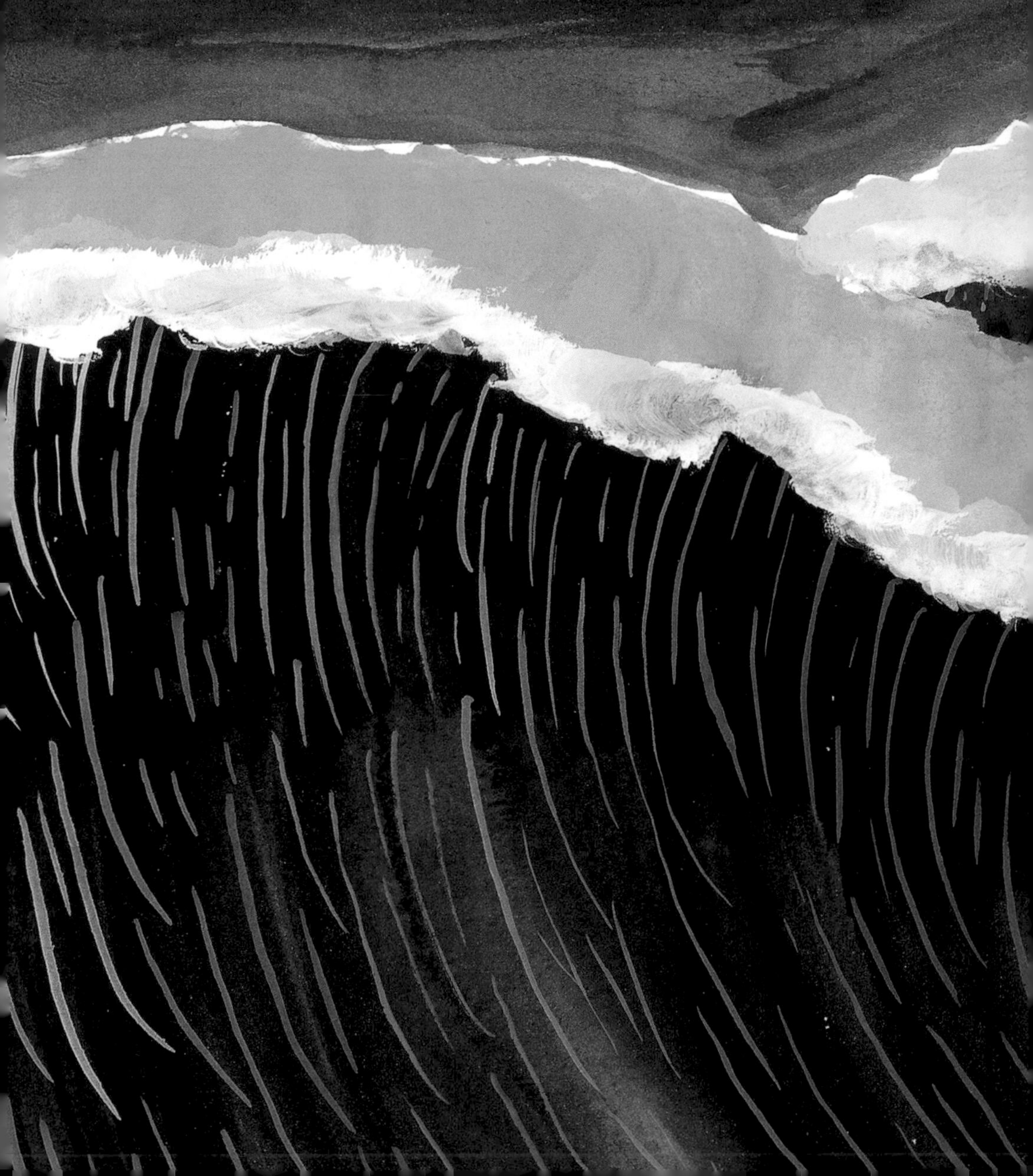

That night, even so close to shore, the poor souls onboard the *Thessaly* were caught by terrible surprise.

The people of Greyshore swore they could hear the pitiful cries carried on the wind as the doomed passengers were swallowed by the mountainous waves.

Jack Cooper lives here, alone,
perched high on the cliffs above the little town of Greyshore.

Next to his house, ringed by a low black iron fence,
is the loneliest cemetery you've ever seen.

GREYSHORE CEMETERY

No one knew how old the little cemetery was. People had stopped visiting it long ago.

A few ancient stones jutted up crookedly, but most had fallen down and were covered with matted grass, lying now deep beneath the snow.

But one stone was always swept clean.

Like his father and grandfathers before him,
Jack was a fisherman on the great lake.

During the winter storms, fishing was scarce.
But Jack hadn't fished in quite a while.

He slept most days and carried a great sadness within him.

He had been on the *Thessaly* that November night, two years before. He was the only survivor.

One person would not let Jack get lost
in his gloom. Her name was Red.
Jack and Red had been friends since
grade school in Greyshore.

Red respected Jack's sadness.

But she was patient, and certain.
She would wait for things to grow.

On a cold morning in March,
Jack heard a knock at his door.

"Well? Don't just stand there!" said Red. "Look at you! You're a mess. Come on, I've got something to show you."

Red grasped Jack by the hand, pulling him out into the winter day.

"Hold on there, Red," said Jack. "Where are we going?"

Red kept walking. "Jack, there's a time to wear a rain hat and overalls, and then there's a time to accompany a nice lady to a nice coffee shop and relax on a nice Saturday morning!"

"But today's Thursday," said Jack. "And there is no nice coffee shop in Greyshore. And like you said, I'm a mess."

Red stopped abruptly and stared Jack straight in the face. "EXACTLY!"

"Could you explain yourself?" asked Jack, rubbing his whiskered face. He was tired and wanted to be back in his house.

But Red turned and kept walking.

"I'm going to open a coffeehouse in this sleepy old town," said Red. "Come on. I'll show you. I found the perfect spot. Old Man Harding is selling his shack."

And off she trudged down the snowy street.

Jack smiled. Red's perpetual enthusiasm was an anomaly in Greyshore.

And so he followed her to look at Old Man Harding's old shack, and his heart became just a little lighter as he walked.

Later that day, as Jack returned home after going to town with Red, he was crossing the little cemetery next to his home and saw something move at the edge of the woods.

Jack's heart skipped a beat; the hair on his neck stood up. Someone dressed in a dark cloak seemed to be standing among the bare trees.

"Hello . . . can I help you?" asked Jack as he approached the dark silhouette.

"I don't remember coming here," said the mysterious figure. The woman's voice was so quiet and sad that it caught Jack's heart like a cold silver hook.

Jack stepped tentatively toward her. "Would you like to come in and sit by the fire?"

"Do you know me?" whispered the woman. The moonlight fell on Jack but cast a deep shadow on the woman, hiding her face.

"No, I'm sorry," answered Jack. "Are you lost? Please, come inside and warm up."

"No," she said. "I cannot."
And she backed away,
disappearing into the trees
and the dark.

Jack shivered and stood for another full minute, looking at the spot where she had been.

The only sound was the waves of the great lake, washing the rocky coast of Greyshore.

OUR
MU
TEA
APPL
BAN
ZUCC
...25¢
...1.50
...75¢
...75¢
...50¢
...1.00

In April the world began to thaw. The ice was coming off the lake, breaking on the rocks. Jack had been in a dark place for many weeks.

Red invited him to see her new coffee shop. It was beautiful. Jack couldn't help smiling. "This is great, Red," he said. "You've done an amazing job with the old shack."

"I know," she answered. "And when we get more customers, you can help me."

Jack frowned. "Oh. But I'm a fisherman," he said. "Not a waiter."

"Not in the winter you're not. You need something to do in the cold months when the lake is dangerous. Anyway, you haven't fished in a long time. You can help me here."

Jack did not know what to say. "I don't know, Red."

Red looked hard at Jack. "What's the matter? You look tired."

"I don't know," said Jack again. "Never mind." He didn't want to tell Red that he often did not sleep at night. He took a sip of Red's fresh coffee, hiding his red-rimmed eyes.

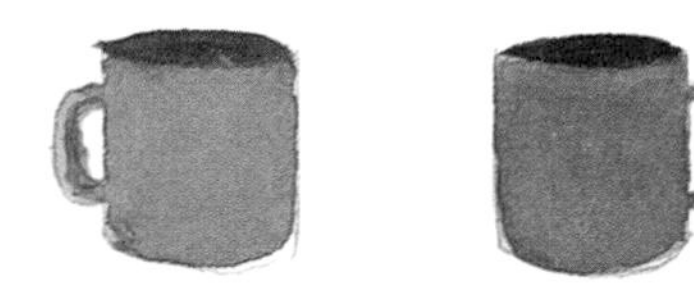

That night, a strange feeling came over Jack when he was at home, like he was being watched. He felt a tingling in his neck. He put his book down and walked to the window. He looked out into the bleak night.

A dark shape stood at the edge of the cemetery, dappled by the darkness and the shadows of the trees. It was the strange woman again—at least Jack thought that it was her.

Jack opened his door and called to her. "Miss! Have you lost your way again? Please come in and get warm!"

"No," the shape answered. "But . . . will you walk with me?"

Jack and the mysterious woman walked along
the black stones at the top of the cliff.
They talked for a long while under the moon.

Even as they walked side by side, Jack couldn't
see her face clearly: she faded in and out with
the changing light as shredded clouds passed
across the thin moon overhead.

She talked softly and kindly to him,
but Jack felt uneasy. He tried not to think this way,
but he couldn't help wonder . . .
the woman didn't seem real.

But that was silly, wasn't it? She was right there
beside him, walking on the cliff next to the great lake
under the moon. She was obviously troubled.
Her words were bereft, and she was so sad and lost.

When they returned to his house and the woman vanished again
into the shadow of the night, Jack wasn't scared anymore—
but he remained a little haunted by something he couldn't understand.

He still did not know her name.

Jack's dreams were dark and stormy that night.

For the first time in many mornings, Jack Cooper woke up eager for the day. Bright and early he bounded out of bed and hurried to Red's coffee shop in Greyshore. He was determined to find the woman he met in the cemetery and help her if he could.

As he walked to town, Jack noticed the ice had left the bay, and he could see open water for the first time in months.

Red's new coffee shop looked colorful and cheery. Jack felt good when he sat down and drank coffee and listened to Red's voice.

But his mind kept wandering to the cliff the night before, and to the unusual woman in the moonlight.

Red stopped talking. She could see Jack's mind was elsewhere, and she took his hand.

"What is it?" asked Jack, looking at Red's hand on his.

"Dear friend, I know you've had it rough. You've had your heart broken." Red took a deep breath. "But now maybe it's time to think about the future and not the past."

"I don't know what you mean," said Jack.

"Maybe you should grab what's alive and real, what's right in front of you, and let go of ghosts."

Jack stood up. "Who says I'm holding on to ghosts?" he said, a little too loudly, and then he stomped out.

Red was alone in her coffeehouse. She looked out the window, hoping Jack would return.

Clouds were darkening the horizon. "Storm coming in," she said to herself.

As the wind outside began to pick up, Red opened an old trunk under the window and pulled out some faded newspapers. She laid them on the counter and began to read.

Two years ago, Jack, his parents, and his bride-to-be, Anne, boarded a supply ship named the *Thessaly* in a large town many miles south of Greyshore.

They were coming back up the shore, returning home with supplies for a wedding, including Anne's bridal gown, when the storm hit that November night.

THES

Oh, never doubt it. Jack did all that he could to save the others. His sailor's skills were good but the water was freezing and the night was so dark. He was exhausted.

Everything was black and silent.

When Jack awoke, he had washed up
on the rocky shore of Greyshore, alone.
His loved ones had slipped away into the cold waves.

Jack was a broken man.

After Jack left Red's coffee shop, he walked down the long road next to the lake. The wind quickened and rain began drumming the docks.
His heart felt as black as the sky.

There she was!

Jack could see the mysterious woman on the curving breakwater that extended from the docks and protected the little bay.

Waves crashed against the grey stones, wreathing her slight figure in spray and fog. She looked out to sea, beyond the breakers, and did not move.

Jack followed her melancholy gaze. His face went pale. He knew where she was looking.

Jack held on to his cap in the wind and crashing spray.
It began to rain harder.

"Miss! Come in from the wall!
The storm is mounting.
You'll be swept over!"

But she would not come in.

Jack stepped out on the quay
and stood next to her.
"You never told me
your name."

"Just remember me!"
she cried suddenly.
"Say my name, then I can go
and be at peace!"

"Go? Where? Tell me who you are!"
Jack was close to her now and
reached for her wrist.

But as he
tried to grasp her,
something odd happened.
He could not grab hold of her—
there was nothing there.
He stepped back, pale as the fog.

"Say it. Say my name," she whispered. She turned to face Jack, and he could finally see her clearly.

"Anne," said Jack.

All around Jack and Anne the clouds rumbled and the waves roared. The rain fell in torrents. But Jack hardly noticed. To him it seemed that the storm was happening in another world.

His beloved Anne stood before him and looked so devoted and sad. His heart was breaking all over again.

"Anne. My Love. You've come back to me," he said.

But Anne shook her head. "No, Jack. I am here only to tell you that I love you, and you must let me go. You must live, Jack."

"But if you love me, then stay!" shouted Jack, and he reached for her again.

But Anne was already fading into the wind. Her black figure hovered over the sea, returning to the site of her drowning.

"Anne! Stay!" shouted Jack, crying. He looked around frantically.

A little boat was tethered to the docks. Jack ran to it and climbed aboard. He released the sail and pushed off into the storm.

Red put the old newspaper clippings back in the trunk. She had to find Jack.

She left the coffee shop and walked briskly along the rough stones that paved the road leading to the bay, oblivious to the raging storm. She had only one thought: she would tell Jack she loved him.

But suddenly she saw Jack in a little boat, bobbing in the dangerous waves, lashed and thrown by the storm.

"Jack!" shouted Red. "What are you doing?" She began to run.

Red's

The storm howled around Jack like a dark beast.

He stood in the little boat, the waves whipping and surging around him. "Anne!" he cried.

He was past the breakers now, right above the resting spot of the *Thessaly*.

Jack's eyes were wild as he searched the water. He screamed into the wind: "Mother! Father! Anne!"

Jack dove overboard, disappearing into the churning waters.

Red saw Jack vanish into the storm-tossed lake.

"NO!" she yelled, running even faster to the edge of the water.

Red searched desperately for a way to reach Jack, but all the boats were crashing and smashing against the docks.

It was hopeless.

Under the surface of the waves, the fury of the storm fell silent. Jack floated gently down. It was quiet and almost peaceful.

A shaft of lightning flashed through the clouds and pierced the waves. Far below him, Jack glimpsed for a moment the *Thessaly*, broken on the deep rocks.

Anne was nowhere to be seen.

"I will join Anne
and Mother and Father,"
thought Jack, closing his eyes.
"This is as it should be."

As his last bit of breath was about to leave him, Jack felt a tug: something was pushing him upward. He heard Anne's soft voice one last time: "Live. Please. Be sad no more."

Jack opened his eyes and looked to the surface. There was light—the sun was breaking through. With a strong kick of his legs and deep pull of his weary arms he pushed himself toward the surface of the great lake.

He broke free from the water, gulped the sweet air, and began to swim.

Anne looked back one more time, then was gone.

Red, her eyes soaked with tears, gasped when she saw Jack emerge from the waves and struggle onto the rocks that ringed the breakwater.

"Jack!" she cried as she clambered down to him. "Are you OK? Jack, speak to me!"

Red helped pull Jack on a wide flat rock, kissing him and crying.

Jack sputtered and opened his eyes. "Red!" he cried, gasping for breath.

And then he kissed her back.

"Do you want to tell me what on earth you were doing out there in that storm?" she said.

Jack returned her steady gaze.

"No," he said.